A DRAGON IN SUMMER

'Now,' said Mrs Green, 'listen hard. On April 23rd, St George's Day, the school is going to do a pageant (that's a play done out of doors) of St George and the Dragon and – Miss Barley has said that Class 4 can play the main parts!'

Scales is determined to be in on the action, but he and his cousin Why Vern have a different version of the ending. There is lots of confusion and fun, with *two* dragons in the battle, an important part for the squire, and a witch to defeat, before the eventful summer term is over.

June Counsel has written four books about Scales the dragon. As a storyteller and lecturer she travels widely, speaking to schools, libraries and children's book groups.

A DRAGON
IN SUMMER

June Counsel

Illustrated by Jill Bennett

GLYNDLEY BOOKS

A DRAGON IN SUMMER

First published in Great Britain by
Faber and Faber Ltd

PRINTING HISTORY
Faber and Faber edition published in hardback 1990
Transworld Yearling edition published 1992
Reissued as *DRAGON IN SUMMER*
in Corgi Yearling edition 1996

This edition Glyndley Books 1999

ISBN   0 9534232 1 2

This book was set in 14/16pt Century Schoolbook by
Kestrel Data, Exeter

Published by Glyndley Books
17 Andrew Close, Ailsworth,
Peterborough PE5 7AD

Printed and bound in Great Britain by
Page Bros (Norwich) Ltd

*To my past and present friends
at Walton Infant
and Walton Junior Schools,
Peterborough*

Contents

1

A Twisted Tail

Oh, what a jubilant back-to-school day! Sam raced down the lane with a lark singing above him in the April sky, his head full of Scales, his heart full of joy. Scales was the baby dragon who lived in Class 4 and whose shiny little head was full of the most super ideas.

He dashed into the playground. 'Hi Weef, hi Bill, hi Chris!' he called as he sped past. The bell rang and he was first in. The classroom was full of laughter and flowers and light. Through the bright chatter nipped Sam into the bay where the big things

were kept. Here, under a table in the window, Scales' cave had been put 'in case there is a chilly day in summer'. Sam knelt down and put his face to the cave's dark mouth.

'Hi Scales! It's me, Sam. Summer's come!'

He waited, eyes sparkling. The cave sat on the floor, dusty, shadowy, cardboard-and-papery. He put his hand in and felt around. He stretched his whole arm in, and drew it out again, dirty with dust.

'Sam, come and sit down, I'm going to take the register.'

Slowly Sam got up and came out of the bay into the classroom and sat down at Blue Table.

'Miss Green,' he began.

Ivy Grubb tossed her ringlets. '*Mrs* Green, silly! Miss is married now.'

'*Mrs* Green then. Scales *is* going to be in this term, isn't he? You did promise.'

'I did, Sam, and Scales can be, if he likes, but when he hears what we're going to *do*, he may not like! Let me take the register and I'll tell you.'

So she took the register, and the dinner register, and sent Tina and Billy Bottom off with them to Miss Barley. 'Now, while we wait, did you all have a good Easter? I did!' And she waggled her new gold ring at them.

'I ate twelve Easter eggs,' boasted Ivy Grubb amid the hubbub. 'Big ones with little ones inside!'

11

'We only eat happy eggs,' said Weefy Buffalo, an odd boy.

Sam sat silent in a bursting impatience. What *could* they be going to do that Scales might not enjoy? Scales was a *terrific* enjoyer. Tina and Billy Bottom came back.

'Now,' said Mrs Green, 'listen hard. On April 23rd, St George's Day, the school is going to do a pageant (that's a play done out of doors) *of* St George and the Dragon and – Miss Barley has said that Class 4 can play the main parts!'

'You mean, St George, the Dragon, the King, the Princess?' shouted Christopher.

'Hush Christopher,' smiled Mrs Green. 'Yes.'

'And his horse?' asked Weefy.

'His horse?'

'St George's horse.'

'That's two parts,' exclaimed Billy Bottom, 'bags I be front end and you be back, Weef.'

12

'I don't know about the horse,' mused Mrs Green. 'I rather fancy St George would dismount before he got to the dragon's lair. Horses don't like the smell of dragon. But you see now,' she glanced at Sam, 'why Scales may not want to be in this term, not if we're to kill a dragon!'

Class 4 were silent. Then Ivy Grubb said, 'We won't tell him, that's all.' She turned to the others and said bossily, 'No-one tell him.'

'Is he here, Sam?' asked Christopher.

'No,' said Sam miserably.

'Perhaps just as well,' nodded Mrs Green. 'We don't want to hurt his feelings. Now, let's go into Assembly and hear what Miss Barley has to tell us.'

Miss Barley told them, amongst other things, that Class 1 being tall, and old, were to be the knights and ladies; that sensible, hardworking Class 3 would be the peasants and market-people; that bouncy Class 4 were to have the speaking parts and the roaring part; and that the Baby Class, being small and so *good* were going to be woodland animals; and that the teachers would sew the costumes and paint the scenery.

Then she sent them out to play, but Sam whipped into the bay and knelt by the cave.

'Scales, do come! I've got something urgent to tell you!'

But the cave, sunk in shadow under the table, was silent. Perhaps it's because he can't feel the sun, thought Sam. He pulled the cave forward and with panting heaves and humps hoisted it on to the table and turned it to face the window.

In the playground, pageant talk was on every tongue.

'We've got the best bit,' laughed Class 3. 'We're going to *do* things. You've got to learn lines.'

'I *can't* kick you,' Billy was saying to Weefy, 'not if I'm in front.'

Christopher tugged at Sam's sleeve, but Sam wrenched away and went over to the railings that ran down one side of the yard, and stood looking through them. The back gardens were as bright as holiday postcards, the one opposite him was so lush it was pushing through the railings and stinging his legs. The first day of summer term and Scales was missing it.

Sam walked moodily down the railings to where the yard ended and the Infant grass began. The may tree! Scales had loved the may tree. Sam ran to it and stood underneath looking up. Bits of blue sky looked back at him through the spiky black tangle, but Scales did not. The bell went. Mrs Green came out. Class 4 went in.

'Sit on the Magic Mat, children. I'm going to tell you the story of St George and the dragon, so that we can start thinking about it.'

'Long, long ago a man was riding
through a rocky desert country, the
country we now call Libya. He was
a Roman soldier and he was called
George. He was also a Christian. He
came to a city called Silene and found
a terrible grief there. The King's only
daughter, Princess Sabra, was going
to be eaten by a dragon that very day.
Even now, she was down by the lake

16

where the dragon lived, waiting. Imagine . . .' Class 4, who could imagine better than telly any day, imagined. They *were* St George, they *were* the Princess, they *were* the crowd. Only at the end when St George swung up his sword and sliced off the dragon's head in the market-place, did Class 4 shout, 'NO!' so violently that Mrs Green jumped.

'He didn't have to kill it,' cried Dinny, 'he had wounded it, and he'd won.'

Little Tina said fiercely, 'If I had been the Princess I would not have

17

used my girdle to lead it back. I would have bound up its wound and made it better.'

'The trouble with you lot,' sighed Mrs Green, 'is that you're all pro-dragon. This dragon was bad. It ate girls. And St George was brave. Now, which of you would like to be St George?'

Only Sebastian put his hand up.

'I see. Well, we'll leave it for the moment, but think about the story. Not all dragons are fun. Now, let's do some measuring. Blue Table, take the trundle wheels. Sam, you be the boy that measures the yard. Take a pencil and a Measuring Card.'

Sam got up and went into the bay. He put his hand on the cave. It was so warm, it was almost hot. He thumped it. 'Scales,' he called, 'Scales.' Not a sound; not a hiss; not a scratch. Dispiritedly, he took a trundle wheel and went out into the yard. He set his back against the wall of the bay and trundled the trundle wheel across until it stopped at the railings of the overgrown garden. What a jungle! What a lovely, lawless mess! Thistles shone, nettles glowered, bushes sprawled and, in the middle, an elder tree leaned over a dandelion lawn. Its trunk was so gnarled and bent it looked as if a dragon's tail were twisted round it. As if . . .

Sam began to tremble. 'Scales,' he called, 'Scales? Are you there? I've been calling and calling down the cave.'

The elder tree shook itself and Scales' voice came sleepily.

'Dragons don't need caves in summer, Sam.'

The tail unwound from the trunk and Scales came rustling down. He flashed over the bright lawn, parted the nettles, looped over the railings and sat down in the playground shining like a thousand milk bottle tops.

'Summer term, Sam,' he beamed, 'and I'm *in it*!'

'But Scales, you may not be, because we're going to do a pageant of St George and the Dragon, and St George—'

'I know that story! Every dragon does. Aunt Spiny told it to me when I was just out of the egg. What's that you've got there?'

'A measuring wheel. I'm measuring the yard.'

'Let me do it,' cried Scales, gripping the trundle wheel in his claws, 'I'm

terrific at measuring. Hop on my back.'

Sam sprang up between Scales' spines and – whoosh – they were off! Up and down, side to side, corner to corner, right the way round and back again whizzed Scales, whirring the trundle wheel beneath him, while up top Sam sang for joy.

'Gracious me, Sam,' cried Mrs Green, when he returned, 'look at your hair! Did you meet a hurricane? But how well you've done! More than the card asked.'

'Scales is back,' Sam told her, glowing, 'and he *does* want to be in this term. He knows the story of St George and the Dragon, though his ends a bit different.'

'Different*ly*, Sam,' said Mrs Green. 'How differently?'

'St George doesn't kill the dragon!'

'No? Who does then?'

'Nobody does. The dragon kills St George!'

2

The Tail Twists Further

'I don't care what Scales says. In our pageant St George kills the dragon,' announced Mrs Green.

'But you said we could write the play,' Class 4 reminded her.

'You can write your speeches, but you can't alter the story.'

'St George could pretend he'd killed the dragon,' suggested Christopher, who was clever.

'And the Princess could back him up,' cried Dinny, who was sharp.

'But they'd be lying,' objected Sebastian. 'I'm not going to tell a lie.'

'Not if she shut her eyes she wouldn't be.'

'Yes, yes,' cried Class 4, beginning to bounce. 'That's it! The Princess shuts her eyes as St George swings his sword up. St George shuts his because – because – because the dragon's face is so ugly. He misses, the dragon runs away, no, no, the dragon *faints*, and St George and the Princess tell the King it's dead because they want to get married and have half the kingdom.'

'St George and the Dragon isn't a fairytale!' cried Mrs Green. 'Good gracious me, did no-one listen yesterday? It's a legend. St George was a Christian, a Roman soldier. He fought the dragon to save the Princess, and he made her lead it back to show it to the people. Then he cried, "Good people, Jesus, the True Son of God, gave me the victory, believe in Him and I will slay the beast." The people shouted, "We will!" So he baptized

24

them all and then he cut off the dragon's head. He had to.'

Class 4 looked doubtful.

'I'll need ten of you to be the dragon's body and someone really clever to be the head that rolls off when St George smites it.'

'Blood ought to spurt out,' said Christopher.

'The neck person could shove the blood out,' said Billy.

Sam and Tina still frowned, but the others began happily discussing the best way of doing blood. The bell went, Mrs Green gathered up her handbag.

'Out to play,' she smiled, 'and keep those ideas coming. We shall need them.'

'Except the one about the dragon killing St George,' remarked Weefy as they went out.

'Where is Scales?' Tina asked Sam. 'We *have* to see him. All the others are wanting to do the pageant now.'

'Come over to the railings of the

empty house,' Sam said quietly. 'Mind the stingers. Now, stare at the elder tree.'

Tina gripped the railings. After a bit she said, 'My eyelashes have got rainbows on them. That tree could be anything, a ship, a witch – oh, oh, I see him! Just his tail twisted round that branch. Oh, dear Scales, but – how can we get to you?'

'I get you to me,' the elder tree said in Scales' drowsy voice.

They felt the railings melt in their hands and themselves drawn forward, the nettles not stinging, the thistles not pricking, until they stood on the dandelion lawn.

They were not in the garden of the empty house, they were in a soft spring wood just starting into leaf. A stream bubbled through, birds fluttered, and Scales smiled at them from an elder tree.

'Welcome to Wish Wood,' he said, and unwound himself.

'But – why are we not on Magic Mountain?' asked Tina. 'Why are we here?'

'You're here because I'm here,' replied Scales. 'Magic Mountain is *mud*. We've got horrible neighbours.'

'Giants, ogres, the Worst Frightener?' cried Sam and Tina, eyes starting.

'No, they're ordinary, they've been neighbours for years. *These* are TWO-LEGGED DRAGONS! Can you imagine it? TWO LEGS! And a spiky silly crest and goggly eyes.'

The children were silent, imagining it. Two legs, well yes, a spiky, silly crest? Scales' crest was spiky, though not silly. Goggly eyes, well, some people have goggly eyes. Christopher often goggled.

'Have you all moved down here?' asked Sam.

'No, only me. The others don't seem to care. My mum says we must accept them because they *are* dragons. My dad's not bothered, because he's big and they're small, and my silly cousins just find two legs funny.'

'We've got two legs.'

'That's different. *Dragons* have *four*.'

'Well, anyway,' said Sam. 'Listen, Miss won't let us do your story, we've got to do hers. Sebastian's going to be St George.'

'And the others want to do it! They are all talking blood,' cried little Tina, distressed.

Scales laughed. 'There'll be no blood! Sebastian couldn't smite the head off a dandelion. Though he might chop his toe off.'

A warbling, burbling sound which was neither bird nor stream began to come through the wood towards them. A look of fury came on Scales' face.

'Hide,' he hissed. 'It's Why Vern.'

He swarmed up the elder tree and lay motionless. Sam and Tina stared towards the sound. Presently, through

the hazel trees came a small, two-legged, goggly-eyed dragon with a silly, spiky crest. It looked like a very large, very odd hen. They smiled, it smiled and said, 'Two of Famous Class 4! Sam and Tiny Tina! Oh, Scales *is* lucky. I wish I had a human. Where is he?'

He swivelled his goggly eyes, one up, one down, then one left, one right. Sam watched fascinated.

'Scales, Scales? Oh, there you are. Aunt Spiny wants you. She's got to pick up a knight.'

Scales came wearily down and turned his face to the children.

'This is Why Vern. Why Vern, Class 4 are *mine*. You're not to play with them.'

He went off and the new dragon stood moving his eyes shyly round and round, this time together.

'Scales has been telling us about you,' began Tina, then stopped, remembering what Scales had been telling.

Sam said quickly, 'You've got a funny name. Why Vern sounds like a question.'

'Why Vern's not my name,' said the little dragon in great surprise. 'Why Vern's what I am. A wyvern, a two-legged dragon.'

30

'Oh, then what is your name?'

The little dragon burbled something that sounded like someone gargling. The children tried to copy, but gave up spluttering.

The wyvern smiled. 'Call me Why Vern. Scales does. Why did you come to see him?'

Both burst into speech. 'Our school's doing a pageant of St George and the Dragon and we want to do Scales' ending where the dragon kills St George, but—'

'It didn't!' cried Why Vern, his eyes going round like catherine wheels. 'Neither of them killed the other! Sit down and I'll tell you the true ending.'

Astounded, the children sat and Why Vern, folding his two legs beneath him, began.

'They had a ding-dong fight, but both having two legs, they were too evenly matched to win, so they cried pax and St George called the Princess (who'd grown bored and wandered off) and the three of them made a plan. The Princess wove a dragon's head out of willow branches and St George fitted it on over the dragon's own head and they led it back to the people and St George smote the false head off!'

'But the people? They must have noticed?'

'They didn't dare come near it! Besides, they were all leaping about and throwing flowers into the air. Then St

George and his squire heaved the dragon on to a cart and the squire drove it back to the forest.'

There was the sound of an enormous splash.

'Ah! Aunt Spiny's dropped the knight she went to pick up. He did a rude picture of her on his castle wall and she saw it.'

The splashing became mixed with shouts.

'But – but, can he swim?' asked Tina, and began to run. Sam sprinted after her, Why Vern followed, flapping his wings and stretching his legs like a racing hen. They came out of the wood to a great brightness: a glittering lake with a knight splashing and shouting in the middle, and Scales on the bank, laughing.

'It's not funny, Scales,' scolded Tina. 'He may drown.'

'It is funny,' chortled Scales. 'And he won't.'

'Here comes his squire,' puffed Why Vern.

A splendid red horse with a boy on its back came galloping up to the lake, its scarlet trappings flapping on its sides. It plunged in and swam towards the knight, who grabbed at its tail and heaved himself up.

'Oh well done, well done!' cheered Sam, while Tina danced with delight.

The horse scrambled ashore, the boy jumped off, winked at Scales and took the horse's bridle. The knight shook his fist at Scales, then hung in a heap on his horse's neck as it trotted off with his squire running lightly beside it.

'I enjoyed that,' said Scales. 'Last time *he'll* chalk Aunt Spiny on his walls. Time you were back, you two, your bell must have gone.'

The children felt the magic tugging at them, the lake, Scales, Why Vern drawing away. Sam remembered something, something that had stuck in his mind.

'Why Vern,' he shouted, '*two* legs?'

The little dragon nodded.

'So it was a—?'

'Yes.'

'Wyvern,' finished Sam, back in the playground.

3

And Grows Longer

Christopher came to school the next day in great excitement with a book under his arm.

'It's my father's. It's got a picture of St George fighting the dragon and the dragon *is* a wyvern. Look!'

'Ugh!' shuddered Tina, turning away. 'How horrible. I don't want to look.'

'He's putting a spear in its eye,' cried Billy, laughing.

'Why Vern's nothing like as big as that one,' said Sam, staring.

Mrs Green came up. 'Oh, Christopher, what a cruel picture!'

'It's very famous,' said Christopher. 'It's in the National Gallery.'

'It's very nasty,' said Mrs Green, 'and the dragon's only got two legs.'

'It's a wyvern,' shouted Class 4, 'a wyvern fought St George and it was a *draw*.'

'Well, you're the dragon experts, but *our* dragon is going to have twenty legs, because there's going to be ten of you inside it. Now let's—'

'He *did* fight on horseback,' interrupted Billy. 'He's doing it in the picture.'

'And he's using a lance, not a sword,' said Christopher.

'I don't want a horse,' said Sebastian. 'Billy just wants to buck me off.'

'Fingers on lips and everyone sitting down,' cried Mrs Green. 'My word! There are lots of pictures of St George and the Dragon and they're all different, because there weren't any reporters or TV cameras then, but *we* are going to have a dragon, a sword, and *if* we have a horse—'

'There ought to be a squire,' interrupted Sam. 'I'd like to be the squire.'

'You can come on behind us, if you like,' said Billy, prodding Sebastian, 'and the horse can fight the dragon. I bet that's what happened anyway.'

Mrs Green went bright red, her eyes shot sparks, she seized the ruler and smote the desk. Golly Moses, thought Sam, she could fight a dragon with a hundred and *fifty* legs and chop it to bits. Class 4 went deathly quiet, sat up very straight and stared with saucer eyes. Icy seconds passed, then Mrs Green let out a long breath.

'That's better. Now let us, in whispers, decide who is going to be what.'

So, in whispers which presently grew to talking, but not to shouting, it was decided that Christopher would be King, Ivy Queen, though she wanted to be Princess ('I've got more jewellery than anyone else.' 'The Princess won't wear *jewellery* to be eaten!'), Nargis would be the Princess with Tina for her maid, Sam could be the squire and skinny Dinny the dragon's head that would roll off.

'Though how we do that I don't yet know,' Mrs Green admitted.

'We do,' chorused Sam and Tina. 'You get bendy willow branches and weave them into a head and fill in the bits between with rushes, and stick stones on with mud for eyes.'

'Sam, Tina, that's brilliant,' cried Mrs Green, glowing a pleased pink. 'The Juniors do cane weaving. I wonder would they weave a head for us? I'll ask at dinner.'

At dinner, the Juniors were enthusiastic and offered to build a cave as well. 'And two of us could be the horse,' they said, 'and St George could ride us.' Mrs Green accepted the cave, but declined the horse.

'Who is your St George?' asked Miss Barley.

'Sebastian.'

'*Sebastian?* Somehow I don't quite see—'

'His mother is making his armour.'

'Ah. A wise choice. You won't forget your corridor pictures, will you, Mrs Green?'

Each class was doing pictures of their part in the pageant to decorate the hall and corridors. The pictures had to be life-size, except the dragon which could be smaller. Sam and Christopher drew round Sebastian and began sticking silver-foil cake cases on for armour.

'That knight Aunt Spiny dropped in the lake, was he wearing armour, Sam?' asked Christopher.

'No, just hunting clothes.'

'Well, when I tell the story I'm going

to put him in armour, because that way he'll drown,' said Christopher.

'But that's not true, and anyway, it's *my* story,' protested Sam.

'Told stories are anybody's,' said Christopher irritatingly, 'not like written stories with authors' names on.'

'Get on, boys, do,' urged Mrs Green. 'Once your pictures are up we can start rehearsing.'

So they went at it, drawing round, cutting out, painting, sticking.

'I'm going to leave St George's face white,' decided Christopher. 'That way he really will look like Sebastian.'

At last the King, the Queen, the Princess, St George, the Squire, the Horse (splendid in red trappings), the Maid, and an immensely long dragon were up in the corridor facing Class 1's snooty lords and ladies.

'Well done, Class 4,' praised Miss Barley, 'but what a pity you forgot to paint St George's face. He's very pale.'

St.
George.

'He's praying,' said Christopher.

'He's praying the dragon won't come,' grinned Billy.

But Miss Barley was looking at Class 1's sneery jeery lords and ladies.

'Now these are bold, brave knights. Just look how confident they are. I wonder they don't go and fight the dragon themselves. They look as if they could eat it for breakfast.'

St George curled slowly forward and fell off the wall.

'He's fainted,' said Billy.

'Don't be silly,' snapped tired Mrs Green. 'Help me stick him back up and then go out to play.'

In the playground the play was no longer St George and the Dragon, but the Knight, the Squire and the Splendid Red Horse, and the story had grown. There was a Faithful Lady in it now, and an island on the lake and a castle on the island. It makes what I saw seem pale and ordinary, thought Sam. He was leaning against the railings, letting his eyes rest on the soothing sprawl of the overgrown garden. He felt a pulling, drawing sensation. The garden seemed to grow bigger. The leaves dazzled and glittered. He blinked.

He was standing by the lake with Scales looking up at him.

'I'm glad you've come,' said Scales. 'I'm hiding from Why Vern.'

Sam sat down and put an arm

between Scales' spines. 'Where is he?' he asked.

'*Miles* away,' began Scales, when a warbling, burbling sound came out of the wood and down came Why Vern with all Scales' silly cousins frisking round him.

'No,' groaned Scales, folding his wings over his head, 'I'm not here. I've vanished.'

But he hadn't and his cousins scampered over to him squealing with joy.

'Scales, and Sam! Scales, where've you been? Why Vern's been hunting everywhere!'

They pounced on Sam. Their little dry claws tickled him as they ran all over him. 'Tell about Class 4, Sam, tell!'

So Sam told about the pageant and when he came to the picture of St George and the Wyvern, the little dragons turned glowing eyes on Why

Vern and squeaked, 'So it *is* true! Oh, Why Vern, you fought a knight!'

'My ancestor did,' burbled Why Vern modestly, but his eyes did a slow dance of pride and pleasure.

'Sam's teacher is having a twenty-legged dragon, so don't think it's going to be anything to do with *you*,' growled Scales.

At once his cousins went bananas. 'Oh, dear Scales, can we go and see it, can we, can we, *please*?' Scales shook his head, whereupon the littlest dragon flew at him and beat him with her tiny claws.

'Don't be a meanie, Scales, let us go, I bet *you're* going.'

Scales looked despairingly at Sam, who said, suddenly, 'Why not? The dragon must have had a family. *All* of you come.'

Squeaks and squeals spiked the air. Jubilant little bodies bounced all over him. Laughing, Sam shut his eyes and pushed them off.

'Hey, hey, leave off, leave off.'

He was back in the playground, leaning against the railings, pushing against Dinny and Billy and Tina and Weefy who had run into him.

'Sorry Sam, we were playing the Splendid Red Horse chasing the dragons.'

'The dragons are coming to the pageant,' Sam told them. 'I've just invited them!'

'Hurray,' cheered Class 4, gathering round, and they went marching in up the corridor chanting, 'The dragons are coming, the dragons are coming. Hurray! Hurray!'

At hometime, Miss Barley, walking down the empty corridor, said to Mrs Green, 'Is it a trick of the light? This morning the knights looked so bold. Now, they look – scared!'

4

A Very Good Point

After the sweat of getting the corridor pictures up, Class 4 swept into the swirl of rehearsals. First they talked about the characters and decided that the Princess would be frightened, but willing, the King would be sad, but resigned, the Queen fussily furious, the Maid loyal and loving and St George—

'How does St George feel?' Mrs Green asked Sebastian.

'Confident,' stated Sebastian.

'And?' queried Christopher. 'He's got to be something else, everybody else is.'

'Lucky,' muttered Billy.

'Clever,' snapped Sebastian. 'He knows how to kill dragons.'

'He doesn't yet,' murmured Mrs Green, 'but he's determined to try. So, clever and determined. Now let's go out and be those things.'

'The Juniors,' said Mrs Green, standing on the Infant grass and waving her arms, 'are lending us their grass for the pageant. So the King's castle will be on *their* grass, the market-place or the wood here in the middle, and the dragon's cave under our may tree. All we've got to do is decide what our characters say and practise coming on and going off.'

'Talking in plays is called dialogue,' announced Christopher, 'but if you make it up as you go along, that's called ad libbing.'

'Thank you, Christopher, that's helpful. Now start ad libbing. Go up to the Queen and tell her that the people are fed up with *their* daughters

50

being sent to the dragon and think it
high time *her* daughter went.'

'Right,' said Christopher, and
marched up to Ivy saying, 'We *can't*
hold our daughter back any longer. It's
not fair.'

'You silly, silly, *silly* King,' snorted
Ivy scornfully, 'of course she can't go,
she's a princess!'

'But I will go,' said Nargis softly. 'It
is right that I should.'

'And I'll go with you,' cried Tina
loyally, and stamped her foot.

'Splendid!' cried Mrs Green. 'Well

done. Now St George and his horse. By the way, I've got a rug at home that will make a splendid horse's hide.'

'Can we have red trappings?' asked Billy.

'My mum can make them,' said Weefy. 'I'll ask her.'

All the mums were helping and Jennie the Helper sat all day in the staffroom whirring the sewing machine. Piles of cloaks and tunics, pyramids of pointy headdresses with floaty veils, bundles of furry costumes with ears, began appearing in the classrooms labelled 'Class 1 Lords and Ladies', 'Class 4 King and Queen', 'Reception Rabbits'.

'Scales ought to see a rehearsal,' said Christopher. 'He might have suggestions.'

'*We* ought to see Scales,' said Ivy huffily. 'He's our dragon. Why doesn't he come?'

'He comes when he wants to,' said Sam.

'Well, we want him now,' said Christopher. 'It's important.'

Chris is getting more kingy every day, thought Sam. I wish I were something more than a squire. He sighed. Sebastian was a most snooty St George. 'All *you* have to do is lead on my horse and stand *back* when I fight the dragon and call me *sir*,' were his orders to Sam.

They were in the classroom trying to settle down.

'Because we must settle down,' Mrs Green said. 'School isn't just fun. It's for doing hard and difficult things so that one day hard and difficult things *are* fun.' And she taught them a hard and difficult thing, how to measure time. 'Now choose a time card and take a tocker or a clock or a sandglass and try to measure time.'

Sam went over to the Measuring Table and chose a five-minute tocker and a card which said, 'How many pencils can you sharpen in five minutes?'

53

He took both into the bay where the pencil sharpener was, started the tocker and began to sharpen a pencil from the box of blunt ones.

The pencil sharpener whirred. Sam took the pencil out and looked at it. 'That's a good point,' said Scales. 'Why aren't you pleased?'

Sam gasped. He was standing by the bright lake beside Scales who was stretched on his back letting the sun get to his tummy.

'I could feel your gloom from here,' said Scales. 'What's up?'

'Chris and Sebastian are up,' said Sam, 'up my nose. Chris keeps putting things in my story that aren't there. He's put an island in this lake—'

'Well, there is one,' said Scales, pointing with his tail, 'round that bend.'

'Oh,' said Sam. 'Oh! Well, he's put a castle on it and—'

'There is a castle,' said Scales. 'Well, a keep, well, a tower.'

'But *not* with a faithful *Lady* in it,' said Sam.

'Why not?' said Scales. 'She's been there yonks.'

Sam was silent, too astonished to speak, cross with Chris for being right, cross with Scales for not telling him. A burbling, warbling sound floated faintly down to them. Scales turned over. 'Quick, get on my back, Sam. Why Vern's coming.'

He slid into the water with Sam gripping his spines. Swish, they were off! It was like riding a speedboat without the noise. All Sam's irritation vanished as spray and air rushed past him.

'There it is,' shouted Scales, doing an enormous swerve, and over an arc of spray Sam saw an island with a tower on top. A figure looked at him from a high window and waved, but Scales skimmed on, then turned and zoomed back to shore.

'Hurray!' cried he, landing. 'Why

Vern's been and gone. There go his clawprints.'

'Oh, but,' cried Sam, 'he's gone with someone. There are hoofprints and footprints. Oh, Scales, let's follow, it might be, it might be . . .'

It was. Racing up the bank they saw Why Vern walking in his bobbing hen's way beside the boy, who was leading the red horse.

'Why Vern,' shouted Sam, 'wait for us.'

The three stopped. Why Vern and the boy turned round and so, after thinking about it, did the horse.

'Why Vern,' cried Sam. 'It's super to see you!'

He meant it was super to see the boy and the red horse, too, but was too shy to say so. Scales came up slowly and sat down at a distance looking dignified and haughty.

'Thanks, dragon,' called the boy.

'What are you thanking him for?' asked Sam.

'For keeping his distance,' answered the boy. 'If he came any nearer, Redgallant here would bolt.'

'But he's not afraid of Why Vern,' said Sam.

'Who would be?' called Scales rudely.

Why Vern burbled gently, 'Redgallant knows me. We're friends.'

The boy looked at Why Vern with

affection, then said to Sam, 'Well, squire, would you like a ride? I'll give you a leg up.'

He hoisted Sam up on to the high red saddle and threaded the scarlet reins through Sam's fingers, then he clicked his tongue and the horse trotted forward. Sam felt his heart bump with excitement. 'Faster?' Sam nodded. The boy began to run, the horse trotted faster. Sam could hardly breathe, the pleasure was so great. It was like music, it was like singing, it was like being king of the world. When they got back, he said as the boy helped him dismount, 'I've never seen a *red* horse before.'

'Roan,' corrected the boy, 'a red horse is a roan. You should know that if you are a squire.'

'I'm only a squire in a play,' Sam told him. 'I'm not clever enough to be a knight.'

'You have to be a squire before you become a knight, and they're not all clever!' said the boy. He stooped and picked up something that had fallen from Sam's pockets. 'Is this a new kind of dagger?'

'No, it's a pencil. For writing.'

'*Writing? You* can write? And read?' The boy looked astounded.

Sam nodded. 'But I'm very slow.'

'*Nobody* reads or writes round here, not even the knights. You *are* clever.'

Sam was amazed at the respect in his face. Why Vern was looking up at him, too, his eyes goggling in admiration, and he saw that Scales had stopped looking haughty and dignified and was shining with pride. Because I'm his boy, thought Sam suddenly, and I can read and write. A glow began to spread through him. I *can* read and write. I am clever!

'Now then, Sam,' said Mrs Green, coming into the bay. 'How many pencils have you sharpened in five minutes? Only one? Oh, Sam! But you have made a very good point.'

5

Two Heads Are Better Than None

'Dress rehearsal this afternoon,' announced Mrs Green, 'and final costume try-on this morning. Look what Jennie's brought!' She and Jennie held up a long silken tube of wonderful colours. 'The dragon's body! Mrs Wong made it and she's put wooden half-hoops inside for the dragon's body-people to hold on to. Remember you're wearing black tights and no shoes. So, carry on with time everybody, Blue Table you can do clocks, and Christopher, come up.'

So Christopher jumped up and tried

on his kingly robes and his kingly
crown, and was promised a beard and
a moustache. 'Two Senior girls are
coming over to help and they'll make
you up. Ivy!'

Ivy marched up carrying a box. 'My
nan's lent me her jewellery for the
pageant!'

'Your grandmother's been very
generous,' said Mrs Green, peering
inside the box, 'but I think we won't

use this rather lovely old brooch. It looks valuable.'

Ivy pouted, but Mrs Green was firm. 'You'll be sparkly enough without it.'

Sam moved the hands of his cardboard clock and frowned. There must be a slow time and a fast time, because yesterday I only sharpened one pencil in five minutes, in the bay, but by the lake I had a conversation with Scales, a water ride, found Why Vern and the boy *and* had a ride on the red horse. Can there be *two* times, going on at the same time, at different speeds?

'Sam,' called Mrs Green, 'are you working? I don't see anything going down on paper.'

'I'm thinking,' Sam answered slowly.

'Good, but put your thinking down on paper. Sebastian!'

Sebastian walked up in a very cocky manner. 'Your mother's made a splendid suit of armour, but what's

this? Sebastian, you can't wear a bow tie!'

Sebastian sniffed. 'I've got to wear it, it's my lucky bow tie. My mum's sprayed it to look like armour.'

Billy snorted, Sebastian whipped round, Mrs Green said quickly, 'Wear it for this afternoon then, but *not* for the pageant. Sam!'

Sam went up slowly. It was hardly worth going up just to try on a cloak and tunic. The door opened silently. A huge dragon's head came in, followed

64

by a horse's head. Scream, scream went Glass 4, gasp, gasp, shriek, shriek.

'Sit *down*, children. Come in, Juniors. Dinny and the dragon people come up.'

Up jumped Dinny, pigtails flying, up jumped the nine who were going to be the body. Into the air rose the dragon's head and out from underneath beamed the sparkly faces of the Vietnamese boat people boys. The horse's head whipped off and there was Youngest Wong from the take-away shop.

'What super, *super* heads!' enthused Mrs Green. 'Oh, lads, you *are* clever! What it is to be Juniors. Try the head on, Dinny.'

Dinny put her head inside and the boat people boys showed her how to hold it on. 'Can you see, Dinny?' The dragon nodded and Class 4 laughed. Then Mrs Green and Jennie helped the nine into the dragon's body. 'Each of you hold a half-hoop above your heads.'

The boat boys held out a tape. 'Mr Cutts sent this.'

' "DRAGON ROARS",' read Mrs Green. 'Well, we were going to do our own roars, but Junior roars must be better. Sebastian, you stand by the door; dragon, over by the window. Jennie, put the tape on, please. Dinny, when you hear the roars, count ten, then move slowly across to Sebastian. There's a place for you to see through in the dragon's neck.'

A low rumbling roar began. Dinny made the dragon's head quiver. The roar grew louder. Dinny moved forward, turning the head this way and that. The roar rose to a bellow, Dinny sighted Sebastian and charged. Sebastian screamed and clutched his bow tie.

'Brilliant, Dinny,' cried Mrs Green. 'Sebastian, you must hold your sword up and be *brave*. Let's have a procession up the corridor, so the dragon people can practise walking.'

So Dinny in the head and the nine in the body, the two boat boys and Youngest Wong proceeded up the corridor, and as they went doors flew open and teachers and children stood up to marvel and cheer the head-makers. Up they went and back they came and as the dragon passed them, the Class 1 knights slithered down the wall and St George's sword fell from his hand.

'We'll have to staple these pictures, Jennie,' sighed Mrs Green, 'they're too heavy for Blu-Tak.'

When they got back to the class-room a loud neigh greeted them.

'Right,' laughed Mrs Green. 'Dragon people have a rest and procession number two form up. Billy, can you see?' The horse nodded. 'Lead on then, squire. No galloping, Billy, just a gentle pacing.'

Sam took the red reins in his hand

and suddenly felt *real*. A squire *is* important. I've got to look after Sebastian and Billy and Weefy. He led them carefully up the corridor, Weefy's little hooves following Billy's big ones, Sebastian marching bravely. Miss Barley came out of her room to praise them and even the fallen-down knights, who looked as though they were taking a lunch break, seemed to perk up as they went by.

They got back just as the bell rang. 'Out to play, everyone. Juniors, thank Mr Cutts *enormously* for the tape and bring your parents to the pageant!'

'We've *got* to see Scales,' Class 4 told Sam. '*Now*.'

'Then hold the railings,' Sam ordered. 'Grip hard and stare at the elder tree.'

Class 4 gripped and stared. The elder tree shook itself and bits began falling off it, only they weren't bits of the elder tree, but Scales' twenty little cousins dropping and sparkling among the dandelions.

'Hey!' shouted delighted Class 4. 'Over here, sillies.'

The little dragons came flashing through the nettles and flying up the railings. 'Scales sent us! We're to do the magic, he's told us how to. First you hold our claws—'

As there were twenty little dragons and thirty-two Class 4 this took some squashing together and several Class 4 legs got stung.

'Now,' said the biggest little dragon nodding at Sam, 'say it.'

'Say what? Oh, you mean—'

'Yes,' nodded the biggest little dragon with shining eyes.

Scales' secret name, thought Sam, tingling. *Sep-dibby-di-dum* – that will bring him to me. 'Shut your eyes, everyone, and shout so you don't hear.'

'HI!' shouted Class 4 as Sam whispered the magic name. Class 4 opened its eyes. The railings were still there.

The littlest dragon turned furiously on the biggest. 'You've forgotten something. I knew you would. Scales should have told me, not you.'

'Shush,' said Sam, 'let me think.' He concentrated fiercely. *Sep-dibby-di-dum* brings Scales to me, but it didn't take me to Scales? Why, of course! Me going to Scales is the other way round, so, I must say it the other way round.

He shut his eyes, pictured the words, then slowly read them backwards. *Dum-di-dibby-sep.*

Whoosh through the railings, whoosh through the nettles, whoosh to the lawn by the elder tree.

'Welcome,' cried Scales, laughing down at them, 'and about time, too.'

'But, but,' cried Class 4, 'it's a different elder tree and it's in a wood and – what's that burbling sound?'

Through the hazels came – 'Why Vern!' shouted Dinny.

The little dragons rushed over to him. 'We did the magic. We brought

Class 4. This is Scales' Class 4.'

'Hello, Class 4,' burbled Why Vern, rolling his eyes, this way, that way, up, down, all ways. 'Lucky Class 4, to belong.'

'Listen, dragons,' said Christopher in kingly tones. 'We're doing the dress rehearsal this afternoon. You must come and watch.'

'We can't this, afternoon,' said

Scales, 'but we're all coming tomorrow.'

'Good,' said Sebastian. 'You'll see me kill the dragon.'

A quiver ran through the dragons. They bunched together and stared at Sebastian. It's funny, thought Sam, Why Vern is right beside Scales and Scales isn't minding.

'Sorry, Scales,' he said, 'but tomorrow St George *does* kill the dragon.'

The dragons looked at him.

'Want to bet?' they said.

6

The Pageant

April the 23rd *came*. Class 4 came to school with colly-wobbles and asked, 'Have you got butterflies in your tummy, Miss?'

'Yes,' said Mrs Green, 'but I've told them to behave.'

'Ours won't behave,' Class 4 quavered.

'They will when the pageant starts. They'll all fly out to watch,' said Mrs Green, smiling as though her tummy were full of delicious pudding.

'Scales is coming,' Christopher said briskly. 'He's bringing his cousins and a wyvern you haven't met.'

'Well, I am surprised,' said Mrs Green, who'd never seen Scales, 'because this is definitely not Dragons' Day!'

Sam was annoyed. If anyone had to tell Mrs Green about Scales it should have been him and he was pretty certain that Scales hadn't wanted Mrs Green to know. I'm too slow, he thought, I should have stopped Chris, he's getting too kingy.

The morning was all churn and bustle – in fact, there hardly was a morning. Playtime was double because Mrs Green and Jennie were helping Mr Duffy carry the props out. Mr Cutts brought his juniors over and erected the dragon's cave in front of the may tree.

'Whew!' whistled watching Class 4, 'that's mega*brill*!'

Big, tall Class 1 brought out the screens they'd painted for the castle and Mr Duffy fixed on the battlements. Christopher grew so kingly

watching this his walk changed to a strut and his chest swelled. Class 2, who were doing the music, brought out their instruments. Class 3 set out their market stalls and helped the Baby Class arrange their woodland trees behind. Then the bell rang and everyone went in and Sebastian said he felt sick.

'You won't be sick,' Mrs Green cheered him, 'because – look what I've brought you. A magic scarf!' She opened her handbag and took out a glittering, green scarf. 'There Sir

Knight, twist that round your neck and wear your lucky bow tie beneath it!'

Sebastian, looking green but not glittering, took it from her with shaking hands.

Then Ivy began to fuss and one of the nine to cry because her mum had given her jazzy tights instead of black ones and panic began to run through Class 4 like a cold running from nose to nose.

'What you can all do,' said Mrs Green, 'is take your felt-tips and draw a terrific dragon. Write its name in jumbled-up letters and we'll ask your parents to puzzle it out while they're waiting.'

So that was something to quieten the butterflies. Class 4 bent their heads and began to draw frantically, fiercely, ferociously and flamboyantly.

Then it was dinner, which Sebastian couldn't eat. Then it was outside with Weefy and Billy practising neighs. Then it was carrying their chairs out and Mr Cutts and his Juniors bringing their chairs over. Then it was the Senior Girls coming over with make-up and giving Christopher a black moustache and quirky eyebrows and Mrs Green and Jennie helping everyone into their costumes. Then it was walking across the playground to the grass with the breeze blowing their crowns and cloaks about.

Dinny and the nine with Jennie and the tape hid themselves in the cave. Mrs Green, Christopher, Ivy, Nargis and Tina sat on chairs behind the castle and the Senior Girls shepherded Sam, Sebastian, Weefy and Billy to a place behind the may tree.

Then there was the noise of parents coming and Miss Barley's voice telling Class 4 parents to pick up 'those flamboyant dragons you see on your chairs and try to guess their proper names'. Then the recorders and tambourines began to squeak and shake, Class 2 began to sing and – and the pageant had *begun*!

'It's all right,' Sam whispered to Sebastian, who was sweating shinily under his helmet, 'we don't go on for ages. Come over here and look at the tangly garden.'

The back gardens backed on to the Infant playground *and* on to the Junior grass. Sam and Sebastian squinted up until they could see the tangly garden's railings. Something bright ran up them, popped over and came scuttling down until it reached the railings opposite the may tree. It was the littlest dragon. She tucked herself into the long grass and waited.

Sam nudged Weefy and Billy with his foot and pointed. They scrambled up and looked and saw nineteen little dragons pop over the railings and scoot down. Billy danced about hugging himself and a pleased smile appeared on Weefy's face.

'That's nice,' he began, 'perhaps—'

'Shush,' hissed Sam, but the Senior Girls were pulling daisies and murmuring about boyfriends, Class 3 were doing their market dance and not a head turned to see Scales come cockily over the railings or Why Vern wander down, one eye goggling at the school and the other taking in the castle and the cave.

The garden behind the railings where the dragons were now sitting was a sinister one, heaped with rubbish, with a witch-shaped fir tree that cast a dark shade.

Billy waved his horse's head at them. Sebastian sliced the air with his sword. The dragons stared back, but neither moved nor uttered.

'Come nearer,' mouthed Billy. 'You won't see it from there.'

'They don't want to see,' jeered Sebastian. 'They know how it ends.'

'You never fight, Seb,' said Billy fiercely, 'and you're not brave. What'll you do if they duff you up afterwards?'

Sebastian stuck his nose in the air. 'Acting's pretend. I *pretend* fight Dinny. They can't duff me up for pretending. Besides,' he added, 'I can't get hurt today.' And he squeezed his lucky bow tie.

Billy stuck his lower lip out and Sam felt sad. It didn't sound very knightly nor very brave nor very anything. He didn't want the pageant spoiled, but it seemed cheaty for it all to be so quick and easy. He looked over at the dragons and saw that they had moved forward and that the fir tree's shadow now stretched almost to the may tree.

Suddenly a horn sounded. The Senior Girls got up from the grass, daisy petals scattering from their skirts, saying, 'Get ready, you're on.'

But Sam had already flung the rug over Weefy and Billy and taken the

reins in his hand. Sebastian gave him a terrified glance.

'What is the matter here? Why are you all so sad?' Sam hissed at him. It was Sebastian's first speech, one he'd made up himself. *'Go on,* Seb, *go on.'* He shoved him forward with his fist and Sebastian marched on, his armour shining like silver, the green scarf floating from his neckpiece. Behind came his sober-suited squire, leading a horse with scarlet reins that neighed and tossed its splendid head.

It was a wonderful entrance. The

parents went wild, the Juniors cheered, Class 4 parents let go of their dragon pictures to clap and the breeze snatched the pictures from their laps and whirled them over to the may tree.

'Look,' cried the parents, 'a flight of dragons!'

Sebastian's mum took her eyes off Sebastian and gasped, 'They're *real*. They're moving!'

'It's the breeze lifting them,' said a mother beside her, 'they've caught on the thorns. Look at your Sebastian, Mrs Brown, isn't he a picture?'

Sam, taking his eyes for a moment from Sebastian's back, saw amongst the flapping pictures and greenbudded spikes pointy snouts and spiky tails and fluttering wingtips.

'Return to your castle, King, return to your homes, people,' declared Sebastian. 'I go alone to fight the Dragon.'

He's left me out, thought Sam with a jolt. He should have said, I and my

faithful squire. The horse gave a scornful neigh and followed Sebastian, stamping its hooves in a menacing manner.

Now the Baby Class brought their trees forward to oohs and aahs and a special clap for a two-legged dragon who was helping them. The dragon goggled its eyes, bowed and vanished. The woodland animals did a hoppity dance and then Sebastian came trudging back followed by squire and steed and explained that he'd had to dismount because the way was steep. The woodland animals hopped up to him, offering him things, and the little dragon hopped out and twitched his scarf away.

'Hey, hey!' shouted Sebastian, jumping up with his bow tie which was on elastic bouncing on his breast-plate. The Juniors roared, the parents laughed, Mrs Brown called, 'Tuck it in, love.' Sam saw Mr Cutts look down his line at an empty chair beside the boatboys, who were laughing like maniacs.

A low rumbling roar began. The Baby Class scarpered. Sam tied the horse to a tree. Nargis, bound to a Junior netball post wreathed with leaves, stared at the cave. Beside her Tina stared, too.

A monstrous head poked out (to a satisfying gasp) followed by a swirly body. It paused, then began to move across on slow, black legs. When the last two legs appeared in jazzy tights, the parents collapsed, the Juniors howled, and the breeze blew three of the pictures off the may tree. 'Oh, oh,' cried the parents, weeping and gasping. 'Oh, oh,' cried Sebastian as, under cover of the pictures, the littlest dragon swooped down and nipped off his bow tie.

'Go on, Sir, go on,' cried Sam, for Dinny had sighted Sebastian and was coming for him. 'Strike now, strike now!'

But Sebastian's sword arm was all astray, his eyes were goggling, his knees buckling. Dinny swung the great head and caught him smack on his helmet. Sebastian tottered and fell. The horse laughed raucously. The Juniors were standing, shouting, Mr Cutts was standing. Sam leapt over Sebastian, drew his dagger (which his dad had made) and plunged it into the dragon's body shouting,

'Die, dragon, die!'

7

Spellbound

'Well,' said Mrs Green. 'Well. I think we need a quiet day.'

Yesterday had not been a quiet day. Yesterday had been as noisy as Bridge Fair. St George had *not* slain the dragon. There had been *two* dragons! A totally unexpected two-legged dragon had interfered with the plot and the squire had killed the dragon. The Vietnamese boatboys had laughed so much they were nearly sick and Miss Barley had had to stand up and calm the parents while Mr Cutts quelled the Juniors.

'Our production has perhaps not

quite stuck to the legend, but then, perhaps, the legend did not quite stick to the truth, but the dragon *is* slain, St George *is* rising to his feet and if you will compose yourselves, we will finish the pageant.'

The parents had sat up straight, the Juniors had sucked in their cheeks, Sebastian had untied Nargis and led her back to Christopher and it wasn't until they were all back in the classroom and all the costumes had been taken off and put away that the losses were discovered. Not just Sebastian's lucky bow tie and Mrs Green's magic scarf, but Ivy's grandmother's brooch (which she shouldn't have been wearing) and Mrs Green's handbag!

It was not in the castle, being dismantled by Mr Duffy, it was not in the cave, being taken down by Mr Cutts, it was not in the staffroom, nor in the staff toilet, nor in her car, it was not *any*where she looked.

'Where is it?' Mrs Green had cried.

'I can't go home without it.' But she had to.

It was still lost and so was the bow tie, the brooch and the magic green scarf. Sebastian was sulky, Ivy was tearful and Mrs Green looked so tired she might have been wrestling with twenty dragons.

'We'll do—' she yawned, 'spelling.'

Class 4 groaned. It did not feel up to spelling. Moan, groan, it went, double moan.

'Moan, groan it shall be,' said Mrs Green, rising to her feet and taking the chalk. 'You said it. Here it is.'

She drew a toothachy face on the board with a speech bubble saying, 'Moan, moan,' and underlined the *o* and the *a*. 'O and a standing together say Oh!'

Then she drew a dragon with a sword stuck in it saying, 'Groan, groan' and St George standing over it in his cloak, and wrote cloak by the cloak and coloured it blue.

89

'How do you spell roan?' Sam asked.

'You mean when a horse is a red colour? That's very clever, Sam. With an o and an a,' and she wrote *roan* on the board and drew a horse and coloured it red.

So they had spelling and it was not as bad as it might be, in fact it was rather good.

When the bell went Mrs Green did not take her handbag, but she did go up to the staffroom and Class 4 went out to play.

But playing was not what they did.

'You silly Sam Luckett,' said Ivy furiously, 'your wyvern stole my nan's brooch!'

'Mr Cutts and Miss think it was Youngest Wong who dressed up as Why Vern, but it wasn't,' spat Sebastian. 'It *was* Why Vern and he's snitched my bow tie and Miss's scarf and he'd better give them back quick or I'll *tell*.'

'Dragon's don't steal things, they guard them,' snapped Sam and swung off to the railings, but Sebastian ran after him and punched him in the back. Then Billy thumped Sebastian and Miss Barley, who was on playground duty, steamed into the fray.

'Knight, squire, steed!' cried she. 'This is not noble. After your high deeds of yesterday and Sam's splendid quick thinking. Gallop over to Mr Duffy and help him pick up the paper petals and – be *useful*.'

So they galloped over to the Infant grass, still strewn with the paper

flowers that Classes 3 and 1 had tossed into the air, and helped Mr Duffy pick them up. When the last petal had vanished, Mr Duffy put his hand into his pocket and pulled out a bundle of drawings and handed them to Billy saying, 'And I don't want to pick *these* up again.'

'Our dragon pictures,' whooped Billy. 'Oh, thanks, Mr Duffy.'

Sam pulled his from the bundle and

yelped. There was an island on it with a tower and underneath *come* written in green letters. The sunlight made the letters dance like green fire and his heart thudded. 'It's Scales,' he said quickly, 'he wants us.'

The bell went and they heard Miss Barley calling. 'After dinner, by the railings,' hissed Sam, 'right?'

Dinner stuck in his throat, but Billy went up for his usual thirds and even picky Sebastian had double pudding. Then they were at the railings, gripping so hard they never felt the stingers, Sam whispered Scales' secret name backwards and – they were there! But not on the lake shore, on the

'Island!' cried Billy. 'There's the tower!'

Sebastian shivered. The island felt cold, though the sun shone and the lake dazzled. There were no trees, only rocks and brambles.

'Scales must be in the tower,' said Sam. 'He's not here. Come on.'

They were almost out of puff by the time they reached the tower and stood looking at it.

'It's miles to that little window,' panted Billy.

'Right, round to the door,' commanded Sam, but there was no door, though they went round twice.

'Scales!' they shouted, 'Scales, where are you?'

Silence. 'It's scary,' whimpered Sebastian. 'I'm going.' He took a step and the rock swallowed him.

'He's fallen down a crack,' cried Billy. 'Here, Seb, reach us your fist.'

They leaned over the crack and reached their hands down to Sebastian, and a whisper floated up from Sebastian's sneakers.

'Class 4? It's me, Scales. The knight captured me and slung me in the dungeon to get even with Aunt Spiny, then he paid a witch to put a spell on the tower so no-one could get in. You must find the unspell quick!'

'How?' they cried. 'Where? There's only us.'

'*Look* for it. She wrote it up somewhere. I heard her scratching.'

They hauled Sebastian out of the

crack and stood staring about them. Where would a witch write? Then Sebastian, always a sharp-eyed lad, yelled, 'I see it. Look at the bottom of the tower.'

Billy stared. 'O' and a step jutted out of the tower and hit him on the kneecap.

'Drag—' began Sam and a second step shot out and touched his shoulder.

'—on,' finished Sebastian and a third step came out, just above his head.

'It's making a stone stairway,' cried Billy.

'I've got it,' shouted Sam. 'It's words

out of dragon! A, an, and, road, roan!'
At every word a step shot out, each
one higher than the last.

'Groan, moan,' called Sebastian,
'dong, dang, dog.' Higher and higher
climbed the steps.

'Man,' bawled Billy, 'gong.'

The stairway stopped.

'No m in dragon,' sneered Sebastian, 'and only one g.'

Billy scowled and pondered. 'Ron,'
he muttered (his dad's name), 'Don,
Dan, Rod' (his brothers' names), 'Dora'
(his sister's name), and beamed to see
a step spring out at every name.

'Go,' screamed Sebastian, 'ago,
God.'

Three steps jutted out.

'Woad,' shouted Sam. No step.
'Goad,' he tried. A step.

'What's it mean?' asked Sebastian.

'I don't know, but it's right for
there's a step.'

On, on they went until the last step
was a leg-length below the window. A

face appeared and gave a cry of delight.

'It's the Faithful Lady,' cried Sam. 'She's climbing out!'

Her skirts hitched to her knees, the Faithful Lady twisted round, and felt for the step below the window. Then she came slowly, steadily, *bravely* down the curving stone stairway. When her foot touched the ground she whipped round and kissed them all soundly.

'Well *done*, my brave young magicians!'

Then she seized their hands and pulled them away.

'But we haven't freed Scales,' cried Sam.

There was a trembling through all the rock. Dust began to fall, stone to slip. The lady cried, 'Behold! The witch's spell is broken and the tower breaks!'

She went skipping down the rocks with Sebastian to the shore, but Sam and Billy pulled from her and leapt into the crack where Sebastian had fallen, wider now, much wider, widening all the time.

'Scales!' they called.

'Coming,' wheezed Scales and came squeezing out like toothpaste, grabbed Sam, grabbed Billy and whooshed them to the shore just as the tower came rumbling, crumbling down.

Dust choked them, dust blinded them. They covered their eyes, their mouths. When they opened them, they were in the playground leaning against the railings, both very dirty, very dusty; Sebastian very clean.

8

Dragons Guard!

The next day felt wrong from the minute it poked Sam awake. His back hurt where Sebastian had punched it. Then when he got to school Ivy thumped him in the chest because he bumped against her, and Christopher attacked him because he hadn't taken him to the island.

'I could have unspelled the dragon spell in *seconds* and I'd have spotted where the unspell was written up quicker than Sebastian.'

Sebastian, pale and wavery and wearing his most aggressive bow tie, started being tiresome.

'The Faithful Lady showed me something *very* interesting, but I'm not telling you what it is until *you*,' he glared at Sam, 'get my lucky bow tie back.'

'Yes, and you can get my nan's brooch back and all,' flashed Ivy.

'I don't know where they are. Why should I?'

'Because your friend Why Vern stole them!'

Sam shrugged. 'Dragons guard treasure, they don't steal,' he said contemptuously.

Ivy tossed her ringlets. 'I bet they steal them first.'

'You put him up to it. He stole my lucky bow tie so *you* could kill the dragon,' shouted Sebastian.

'I say, that's clever,' cried Christopher. 'Did you, Sam?'

'I s-saved *you*. You were d-down,' Sam said, stuttering with rage. 'The d-dragon would have *crushed* you.'

'I was just getting *up* and you spoilt it!' Spitting with fury, Sebastian lashed out. Sam shoved him back so hard he fell over two chairs and landed on the floor.

'Ooh, Sam Luckett, you *bully*,' squealed Ivy and squealed again as Sam hit her.

'Go on, Sam, go on,' cheered Billy.

'Don't, Sam, stop!' begged Tina.

'*Every*body stop,' exclaimed Mrs Green, walking in. 'Goodness gracious me, Sam, what *are* you doing, punching Sebastian and hitting Ivy?'

That's what I'm doing, thought Sam crossly, punching Sebastian and hitting Ivy, but he said nothing.

Mrs Green surveyed them. She looked tired herself. 'Well, Class, this is what's called reaction. We've had a tremendously exciting day with the pageant, then a hard day of clearing up, and some of us are worrying about lost things, and now we're frazzled!

So, sit down, quietly, and Sam, you'd better go and sit under the clock until playtime.'

Scowling, Sam walked up the corridor. St George smirked at him in a very Sebastianish manner. He sat down on the cushion under the clock and settled his bruised back against the wall. All around him on low tables and shelves were plants, a rubber plant, a cheese plant, not looking like rubber or cheese, and a trailing frothy plant like a green mist. He could hear the Baby Class being told a story and wished he could make out the words. The corridor was full of cool sweet air,

because the door at the end stood open. He could see like a tiny bright picture the Junior grass shimmering like silk and the seven trees that marked the boundary between the Junior grass and the Seniors. A wispy tree, a muddly tree, a pointy tree, a round tree, then a gap, then a silver-green tree, a burnished red tree, and one ordinary tree.

The seven trees drew his eyes, the Baby Class murmur soothed his ears. A spider plant leaned over and tapped him on the shoulder.

'Message,' it said, and tapped gently on a shell.

All round the cushion under the clock were interesting things, shells, coloured bottles, a family of stuffed hedgehogs on loan from the museum, to take your mind away from punching people. Sam picked up the shell and held it to his ear.

'Bit of magic coming, Sam,' warned Scales' voice.

'Shift yourself,' said the spider plant impatiently.

Sam got off the cushion and the four plants began to move their leaves, the shells started to hum, and slowly before his eyes a boy dressed in his clothes with a scowling face appeared cross-legged on the cushion.

'That's not me,' exclaimed Sam, shocked.

'We know it's not you,' snapped the spider plant. 'You're you, but it's a jolly good likeness. Now get along. Scales is waiting.'

Sam sped down the corridor feeling so light he hardly touched the floor. Out of the door, down the steps, over the grass to the burnished tree. It was like being drawn along by an invisible thread very fast. As he got near the gap he saw beyond the seven trees more and more and more trees. Then he was amongst them, the speed stopped, he was in Wish Wood looking at Scales.

'Jump on,' said Scales, turning as he spoke. Sam was still clambering on when Scales was out of the wood and in flight. Oh, how good it was to be flying! How the air sang and the sun shone and the lake raced away beneath him.

'Going down,' sang out Scales. Down they swooped, landing on the island among the tumbled stone of the fallen tower.

The lady came running up to them, holding out something and talking fast. 'Please, please take this picture back to the knight's castle, *my* castle. It is my son. He was only seven when the knight captured my castle and stole it from me. My son may still be there. He will have a scar on his chin where he fell down some steps.'

'Come with me,' invited Scales.

'No, no,' laughed the lady. 'I am too big, besides I would not be comfortable on your spines. Find my son, get him to bring a boat over, quickly.'

'Why Vern will help, won't he, Scales?' said Sam.

'That useless two-legged thing,' snorted Scales. 'He's vanished! Jump on my back, Sam.'

'No,' said Sam, surprising himself. 'I'll stay with the lady.'

Scales shot him a pleased look and flew off, holding the picture in his claw. The lady gave Sam a hug and a kiss. I wish she wouldn't, thought Sam, though he liked her.

'Come,' she said, 'I will show you where there is a spring of sweet water. I found it last evening and you shall tell me about yourself. It is ten years since I last had a boy to talk to.'

She took Sam to a little spring bubbling up from the very heart of the rock and while he drank told him how she had come to be shut up in the tower.

'Your brother!' gasped Sam. 'The knight is your brother?'

'Yes,' sighed the lady. 'He was

always greedy and – hark! I can hear voices! Oh, Sam, Sam, it is the knight, my brother, and the witch coming back.'

Peering over the cliff edge they saw a boat coming nearer and nearer with the knight in it and a hunched black figure.

'Nowhere to hide, no weapons,' moaned the lady.

'Crouch down,' commanded Sam, 'they won't look here. Anyway, they'll think you're dead under all that stone.'

They crouched down, much bothered by the brambles, but too scared to mind. Then they heard the scrape of feet on the rock and the panting breath of those who climb. What I'll do, thought Sam, is grab the knight round the legs and topple him over. 'You rush at the witch,' he whispered to the lady. She nodded, lips pressed tight. Then two legs appeared before him, a bellow sounded above

him, and before he could do anything
he and the lady were hauled to their
feet. The lady fought and hit, but
the knight held her fast. Sam tried
to topple him, but the knight only
laughed.

'Now, witch, spell me these two into
frogs.'

The witch began gathering things. 'Hurry,' said the knight. The witch crooned an up-and-down song. Sam saw strange eyes behind the veil. The witch hobbled down to the shore for five different shells and seven different seaweeds. 'Get on,' snarled the knight. The witch drew a pointy pattern in the dust, then went wandering off to find nine different herbs. '*Frogs*, I said, not elephants,' raged the knight. The witch put all these things in a bucket of spring water and collected sticks for a fire. 'Come *on*,' groaned the knight.

The fire began to spit and spark, the witch began to stir and sing. But I can hear *another* noise, thought Sam excitedly, a noise from the shore.

The witch started singing at full screech, but the other noise grew louder. The knight heard it and snatched out his dagger. The witch sprang at him, cloak and veil falling away.

'Why Vern!' shouted Sam.

'Reptile!' screamed the knight as he drove the dagger into Why Vern's shoulder instead of the lady's chest.

'Sam, Sam.'

Somebody was shaking him, somebody was waking him.

'It's all right,' said Sam, opening his eyes. 'Scales and the boy got there just in time.'

'Well, I'm glad,' smiled Mrs Green, 'but come down to the classroom now and see what nice things have happened.'

Sam got up off the cushion and followed her. What a difference in the classroom. Smiles everywhere, Sebastian smirking, Ivy beaming. And on Mrs Green's desk—

'Yes,' said Mrs Green. 'Mr Cutts' Juniors have been over. You remember we took the pageant dragon over to them in a big bundle? Well, as they were straightening it out this morning, out from its folds fell – *my* handbag, *my* green scarf, Sebastian's lucky bow tie and Ivy's grandmother's brooch!'

9

Scales' Dad Says Thank You

Spring rushed into summer. The elder tree in the overgrown garden covered itself with saucers of tiny white flowers and the dandelion lawn became a sea of buttercups. May Day came; the photographer came; the Junior School Fête and the Sponsored Walk came. Class 4 were so busy they almost forgot Scales, until one day Nargis came in smiling and swinging her long plait.

'I've just seen Scales! He said, "Playtime railings, quick!" '

So at playtime Class 4 rushed to the railings and found Scales sitting comfortably in the brambles.

'We've been busy,' Class 4 told him, glowing and panting.

'So've I,' replied Scales. 'Summer's castle-capturing time among the knights and there've been wild doings round the lake, but listen, Sam, my dad's so grateful to you and Billy and Sebastian for rescuing me he wants to do something nice for you.'

'Ooh!' said Class 4 enviously.

'Something big?' asked Billy, eyes sparkling.

'Something for all of us?' suggested Sam, seeing how the others looked.

'S-something safe, I hope,' stuttered Sebastian.

'All three,' Scales nodded. 'It will be on Midsummer Day, because that's the only day magic enough to hold my dad.'

He turned, swished through the buttercups and vanished into the elder tree.

Class 4 began to buzz. 'He'll give us

gold and jewels,' cried Ivy. 'Something ordinary, but nice,' whispered Tina. 'Dreamy and magical,' smiled Nargis. 'Clever,' stated Christopher. 'Athletic,' hoped Dinny Delmont who was forever climbing things. Sam had no ideas and Weefy said, 'It'll be unexpected.'

'I might as well be a postman as a teacher,' said Mrs Green, 'all the letters I have to give you to take home. This one's to tell your parents that our outing will be on June the 24th—'

'June the 24th?' echoed Christopher.

'June the 24th,' repeated Mrs Green. 'Midsummer Day.'

'But we won't be here!'

'No, Christopher, we will be at Hunstanton having a picnic by the sea.'

'We'll have to tell Scales,' said Christopher gloomily at dinnertime. 'Perhaps his dad could come in the evening when we get back.'

They went over to the railings.

Something glittered among the brambles. It was the littlest dragon.

'Scales,' it began, but the boys interrupted.

'Tell Scales, we're going to Hunstanton on Midsummer Day. We're going to have a picnic . . .'

'Right,' snapped the littlest dragon, whisked and went.

The next morning Sam went to the railings by himself. As soon as he touched the railings the white saucers on the elder tree began to jostle. Scales' voice came to him, rather muffled.

'My dad says the picnic's on him.'

Puzzled, Sam went in and told the

others, 'Scales' dad says the picnic's on him.'

'But what's he *mean*?'

'He *means*,' explained Christopher, 'that he'll pay for it. If you say something's on me, like the party's on me, you mean *you* will pay for it.'

'So our mums won't have to pay?'

Class 4 began to speculate. 'Perhaps he'll leave a sack of gold at the school, or make our dads win the pools, or our mums win at bingo.' In the end they asked Mrs Green. Mrs Green was firm.

'*No* sacks of gold will be accepted. Your *mums* will pay for the coach. Your *mums* will pack you up a picnic lunch in a tin with your name clearly on it and put your drink in an unbreakable container with your name on it and no more than a pound pocket money in a purse with your name on it. *That* is what will happen.'

'It won't in our house,' remarked Weefy, 'because my dad will do it.'

Speculation continued. Scales did not reappear nor were there any more messages. Nobody's dad won the pools, nobody's mum won at bingo. The mums paid for the coach (though dads were out of work) and Midsummer Eve arrived.

'You realize that *this* is the real magic time,' Christopher remarked, 'when you're supposed to see The Wild Hunt and fairies and witches—'

A pang struck through Sam. Walking home through the lane the word witches stuck in his mind. He heard a cackle close to his ear though nobody was near him. Of *course*, he thought, the *witch*! The witch whose spell we broke! *She'll* try to spoil the picnic tomorrow.

Midsummer Day dawned white, cold and damp. Class 4 shivered on the pavement and waited for the coach; and waited. At last Mrs Green went into the school and rang up the coach office who told her the driver was sick and they were finding a relief. Ha! thought Sam, the witch strikes! Eventually the coach came and Class 4 climbed aboard; a small class, some were already holidaying with their parents. Miss Barley came, and Jennie and Mrs Brown. Sam quite expected the coach not to start, but it did.

Mist lay over the flat fen country and the coach went slowly. They stopped at Sandringham to go to the toilet. 'There,' said Mrs Green, pointing, 'that sign that says LAVATORIES. The Queen doesn't say toilets.' They looked at the tremendously tall gates with dragons and shields on top. How proud Why Vern would be, thought Sam, if he could guard a gate like that. They raced about the Kickabout Area to stretch their legs. From behind the dark red trunk of a Norfolk pine Sam heard a cackle and his spine chilled.

The mist lifted and they saw the

small green hills and dark brown cottages of Norfolk, but they didn't come to the sea, because the driver stopped and said, 'I'm lost. I thought I'd take you the pretty way, but now I don't know where we are!'

She strikes again! thought Sam, and felt worried.

But Miss Barley took the map, sat by the driver and directed him. She turned him right, she turned him left, and righting and lefting she got him out of the web of little lanes he had got into and back on the road to Hunstanton.

They were there! Late, hungry, but *there*, smelling the sea, wild with excitement.

'Now,' said Mrs Green. 'We'll have our picnic.'

So they sat on the green cliff top eating and drinking, then they went down to the beach.

The sea was so far out they could hardly see it. The little low cliffs were banded red and white and between them and the far-off sea was sand and sand and sand. Damp sand for making castles, ribbed sand for running on, dry sand for sitting in. The sea had been on the beach at some time for there were rock pools pleading to be paddled in.

Black-headed gulls swooped above them, white-headed seabirds watched from the cliffs. The day was so high and blue and shining, Sam thought, the dragons are fighting the witch and winning, but he was sorry the picnic hadn't been on Scales' dad.

When they were all wet to the waist, Mrs Green called, 'Run about now until you get dry, because we're going home soon.'

So Class 4 raced along the dry sand near the cliffs until the cliffs sank down to mere banks and the sand was heaped up in wind-blown dunes with marram grass growing on them.

'Look at that *whopper*!' yelled Billy

Bottom and raced towards an enormous dune, curved and hollowed and twisted. Class 4 raced after him and up and up they climbed until they were sitting on the top between

tall spiky ridges.

'Well,' laughed Miss Barley, 'that is for *young* legs. You and I, Mrs Green, will sit here. Jennie, if you and Mrs Brown go round to the other side we

shall be able to keep an eye on the children.'

Jennie and Mrs Brown walked round to the other side. Jennie spread out their rug, but Mrs Brown went to the foot of the dune and called up.

'Sebastian love, come and take this. Someone left it on our doorstep.'

Sebastian slithered down, took the tin, yelped, and climbed back.

'It makes my fingers tingle!'

It was a green tin with a label which said FOR THE PICNIC. He opened it. A gorgeous smell came out.

'*Cakes*,' sighed Class 4. Sebastian passed the tin along. 'M'm,' smiled Class 4, munching. There were seconds and thirds and 'Oh,' said Sebastian, 'there's plums at the bottom.' Golden, juicy plums. Class 4 sat on the spine of the dune like birds along a roof ridge feeling – *magical*. Presently Billy drew in his breath sharply, 'Look here.' He'd been moving his heels back and forth and the sand had fallen away. Class 4 looked and saw, not more sand, but – a shining dark green scale. Then Sam knew. Class 4 rubbed bits of sand away, pulled bits of grass up and found a red or purple scale, a dark red spine, the rib of a folded wing.

'Careful,' warned Sam, but he didn't need to. All knew that the discovery was too precious to spoil by any silliness.

'How good the children are being,' said Miss Barley. 'I thought they'd romp all over that sand dune.'

'They are romping a little,' said Mrs Green.

'Yes, but so carefully.'

The coach broke down on the way home, but nobody whinged, nobody was sick. Witch, thought Sam, give up, go home, you've *lost*!

As he thought this a lorry stopped, the driver leaned out. 'Want any help, mate?'

When at last they were on their

way, the Midsummer sun was setting in a pageant of fiery colours and fantastic shapes.

'Now,' said Miss Barley, 'it's been a long day and Mrs Green and Mrs Brown and Jennie and I are very tired. You may sing so long as you don't bawl or you may talk quietly.'

But Class 4 didn't sing, didn't talk, but sat watching the sunset, seeing what the teachers with their eyes closed couldn't see, Scales' dad flying, slowly, grandly, magnificently home.

10

The Hardest Word

It was almost the end of term. The two top classes were over at the Juniors seeing where they would go next term. Squeaky little brothers and sisters were being shown the Baby Class. Class 3 were in Class 4's room and Class 4 were in big, high-ceilinged Class 1's room, which was the oldest part of the school, because Class 4 would *be* Class 1 next term.

'We'll have Miss Barley,' whispered Class 4, feeling frightened and excited at the same time.

'Ah, no, that's what I must tell you,' said Mrs Green, 'you won't. Miss

Barley has got to do more administration, that's running the school, so *I* am going to have Top Class!'

Class 4 stared, unable to imagine Mrs Green as Miss Barley.

'*Can* you do the New Maths?' asked Christopher.

'I shall try,' said Mrs Green stoutly.

'*And* Top Level Science?'

Mrs Green clutched her head. 'Yes!'

'*And* French?' went on Christopher. 'Because of the Tunnel?'

'Will you have to teach *French*?' asked Class 4, awestruck.

'Who knows what teachers will have to teach next?' said Mrs Green gloomily.

'You could teach anything,' said tiny Tina.

'And if you can't, we won't let on,' said Billy Bottom.

'Thank you,' said Mrs Green. 'With your cleverness and my efforts we shall get through. Can anyone read that notice?'

130

She pointed to a notice which said:

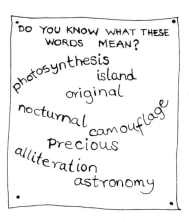

All round the notice Class 1 had stuck up explanations of what each word meant.

'That's wrong,' said clever Christopher, pointing to one. 'Nocturnal doesn't mean the hind part of an elephant! It means night.'

'They're very hard words,' said Sam, who could only read *island*.

'We shall learn harder ones,' said Mrs Green, and she seized a chalk and wrote *application, concentration, intellectual, triumph, nonpareil* on the board. 'The last one's French,' she said.

'We'll have a competition,' decided Christopher, who was a great one for competitions, 'to find the *hardest* word and *say* it.'

Sam gazed about him, it was like a church or a hall or a barn. A hundred years ago it had been the whole school with a bell on top to ring the children to lessons and fields all round. The children had written on slates sitting on forms with a grumpy iron stove to keep them warm. I'd have managed then, thought Sam, who never felt clever, though he sometimes felt sure.

At playtime he wandered over to the railings and stopped, shattered. A man was in the garden scything down the nettles. The brambles were already gone and the buttercup lawn had been mown.

'You aren't going to cut down the elder tree, are you?' asked Sam in agony.

The man glanced at him.

'You can make wine from the flowers and from the berries,' Sam told him.

'It's a weed,' the man said. 'It's coming down.'

How awful, thought Sam, suppose I call Scales and he comes and the man decides to cut down the elder tree and slices Scales in half. Oh Scales, you're in *danger*! The white saucers on the elder tree bobbed up and down. Scales' laughing head pushed through.

'What's up?' asked the man. 'What are you grinning at?'

'I-I,' stammered Sam.

Scales shot a very bright glance at the man who suddenly bent down muttering, 'More rubbish, broken glass, tin, plastic—'

'Oh, give it to me,' Sam cried, 'it's *beautiful*.'

He stretched his hand through the railings and the man put a curved, flattish, thin thing that glittered all colours in his hand. It was neither glass nor tin nor plastic nor any substance made by man, but a dragon's scale as Sam had seen at once. It was so lovely he shut his eyes to feel it better. When he opened them he was standing by Bright Lake with Scales looking at him.

'Hurry, Sam, something very important's happening and I want you to see it.'

Sam climbed on and Scales flew inland until they came to a castle with a faint rude picture of Aunt Spiny on the walls. Outside the castle a ring of people had gathered. The King and Queen and Princess were seated on a dais and Aunt Spiny and Scales' little cousins were sitting facing them with the people keeping a respectful distance on either side. In the space in the middle stood the Faithful Lady opposite the Bad Knight and behind her Sam could see Why Vern and the Splendid Red Horse.

'What's happening?' asked Sam as they landed.

'The Knight's got to say the Hardest Word,' said Scales with satisfaction.

'The hardest word?' repeated Sam.

'If you really mean it,' replied Scales.

Sam stared at the Knight. He looked most uncomfortable. His face was red, his brows drawn together in a terrific frown. He looked as if all his clothes hurt. Everyone's eye was on him. Even Why Vern's eyes were *both* fixed on him.

'Let the Knight say the Hardest Word,' called the King, 'and let all hear it.'

The Knight opened his mouth, quivered his lips, then shut them. He can't say it, thought Sam. The Knight tried again. Hoarse sounds came from his throat, but they didn't make a word. Golly, thought Sam. The Knight whispered a tiny word that sounded like a hiss.

135

'Louder,' commanded the King.

The Knight said it again looking at his toes.

'Once more,' ordered the King, 'and LOOK UP!'

With a great effort the Knight raised his head, looked his sister in the eyes and said, as though strangled, 'Sorry.'

The Lady held out her hand, the

crowd cheered, the Splendid Red Horse was led forward by a splendid young man with a white tunic over his armour and a shield on his arm, and emblazoned on the shield and embroidered on the tunic was—

'WHY VERN!' cried Sam in delight.

—a two-legged dragon with a dagger piercing one shoulder, for the boy was a groom no longer, but a knight!

The castle gates swung open. The King and his Court rose and walked towards them followed by the Faithful Lady and the Contrite Knight (that means sorry), but the Red Knight and Why Vern came over to the dragons.

'I've come to say goodbye,' said Why Vern, smiling his gentle smile. 'I serve the Red Knight now. Good-bye dear Fourlegs, thank you for a lovely summer.'

Scales growled and looked at his claws. Sam looked at him. The Knight and the horse looked at him. Aunt

Spiny and the cousins closed round them in a ring. Aunt Spiny hissed, 'Stay, Why Vern, Scales has something to say to you.'

Scales spluttered and stopped.

'Go on,' whispered Sam, '*say* it, you were rotten to him, you know you were.'

'I can't,' muttered Scales. 'I want to, but I *can't*.'

'The Knight did it,' urged Sam. 'You can't be beaten by him!'

'We'll help you,' cried his cousins. 'We'll say it with you.'

'No, you won't,' snapped Scales, his head coming up with a jerk. 'I'll say it myself. SORRY!' he roared so fiercely Why Vern jumped.

Then he said, 'Truly sorry, Why Vern, you *are* a dragon. One of us.'

Why Vern blew out a puff of smoke that made Scales jump backwards.

'No,' he burbled, eyes goggling merrily, '*you* are one of *me!*' And he flew off.

Then all the dragons burst into leaps and laughs and Sam flung his arms round Scales. 'Oh, Scales, well done, I do love you!' Bells began pealing from the castle and—

'I don't know what you're laughing about,' said the man, 'but your bell's gone and you should be in.'

Sam went dancing in and won Christopher's competition to Christopher's annoyance.

'It's *the* hardest word to *say*,' Mrs Green told them, 'if you mean it.'

On the last day Sam went to the

railings dreading what he would see. The garden was unrecognizable, the paths weeded, the beds planted, the lawn plain green, but the elder tree still stood and as he looked it shook itself and Scales slid modestly out of it and came over to him.

'Oh, Scales, I'll be Top Class next term. Mrs Green's moving up too, but I don't know whether she'll let you in because—

'Top Class!' exclaimed Scales, all his old bounce returning. 'Of *course* I'll be in it! Dragons *are*

TOP CLASS!'

THE END